Captain Flinn
and the
Pirate Dinosaurs
☠ Smugglers Bay ☠

Written by Giles Andreae

Illustrated by Russell Ayto

PUFFIN

SMUGGLERS BAY

For Elwen – G.A.
For Pirate Loveday – R.A.

PUFFIN BOOKS Published by the Penguin Group: London, new York, Australia, Canada, India, Ireland, new Zealand and South Africa. Penguin Books Ltd, Registered Offices: 80 Strand, London WC2R 0RL, England puffinbooks.com First published 2010. Text copyright © Giles Andreae, 2010. Illustrations copyright © Russell Ayto, 2010. All rights reserved. The moral right of the author and illustrator has been asserted. Printed in China.   ISBN: 978-0-141-50132-1
007 - 10 9 8 7

"Here we are," said Miss Pie.
"Welcome to **Smugglers Bay**."

"Please, Miss," said Flinn, who was wearing
his favourite pirate captain outfit.
"Why is it called Smugglers Bay?"

"Well, in the old days,
pirates used bays such as this for smuggling
all sorts of naughty things in and out of their dens,"
explained Miss Pie to the class. "But everyone knows
that pirates don't exist any more."

"Now remember!" said Miss Pie. "Whoever does
the most interesting drawing will have it pinned
on the school noticeboard for everyone to see!
Right then . . . off you go!"

"Hey, Flinn, what's that?"
said Pearl, pointing to a
shape in the sand.

"It looks like a
footprint,"
said Flinn,
"but it's huge!"

"There are some
more!" said Tom.
"Let's follow
them."

Soon they
came to a cave but,
at the back of the cave,
the footprints stopped.

"What's this?"
said Violet, looking at
a rusty metal bar
sticking out of the rock.

Doo noT tuch
thIS leEver.
It duz NOT leeD
to a sekrit PASSige.
So GO awAYE!

"Let's see what it does!"
said Flinn. As he pulled the bar,
there was a loud creaking noise.

"A secret doorway!" said Violet.
"And look! There's a passage behind it!"

The children
all clambered

down the passage

and came out
at the edge . . .

. . . of a gigantic cavern.

"Pirates!" gasped Flinn.
"But they're not just ordinary pirates.
They're our old arch enemies . . .

PTERODACTYL

The dinosaurs were surrounded
by lots of small wooden trucks.
And into these trucks the dinosaurs
were piling giant shovelfuls of
stinky, squishy, slippery . . .

"SAUSAGE MEAT!"
boomed a loud voice behind them.
"FOR MAKING SCRUMPTIOUS
PIRATE SAUSAGES!"

STEGOSAURUS

It was the ferocious
Captain Tyrannosaurus Rex.

"Didn't you know they're
a dinosaur's favourite food?
And you little scallywags have
appeared just in time to make my
favourite sausages of all . . . scrumptious
CHILDREN CHIPOLATAS!"

He grabbed Violet under one scaly arm and leapt into a passing truck.

"Come on, gang!" shouted Flinn. "Let's follow them!"

The truck sped
over the tracks,
twisting through
dark narrow tunnels . . .

Clickety-clack

Clickety-clack

Clickety-clack

. . . and in the distance ahead of them,
the children could hear the T. Rex singing,

"Sizzling sausages squished in a bun
I long for that tingling taste on my tongue.
Nicey and spicy or cucumber cool
Oh, sizzling sausages do make me drool!"

Suddenly, Captain Flinn and his friends

were catapulted high into

the air and

landed with a

THUMP

on their bottoms beside

a secret lagoon.

There in front of them was a huge
pirate ship and rowing towards it,
with Violet tied up behind him,
was the Tyrannosaurus Rex.

"We've got to save her,"
said Captain Flinn.

"Come on!

We're going to

have to swim!"

The children clambered
up the side of the ship.
On the deck was the
hugest, noisiest
contraption that they
had ever seen.

The Pirate Dinosaurs were piling great loads of sausage meat into the machine and out of the other end plopped giant, slimy, pink sausages.

As they worked, the dinosaurs began to sing:

"Sizzling sausages squished in a bun
I long for that tingling taste on my tongue.

Nicey and spicy or cucumber cool
Oh, sizzling sausages do make me drool!

But something that makes
my mouth get even wetter
Is yumptious young children!
They taste so much better!

Roasted or toasted or frittered or fried
Sautéed or scrambled or pancaked or pied

Covered in ketchup and served on a plate
Especially their giblets – oh, crikey, they're great!

But what is the dinner that nothing can beat?
A pirate girl sausage is quite the best treat!"

Captain Flinn ran to the sausage machine, but Violet had already disappeared.

He stuck his cutlass hard into the contraption.

CLANK!

SPLUTTER!

SPLAT!

"You're too late!" roared the T. Rex, lunging at Flinn with his dagger.

"Yo ho ho!
Yo ho ho!
Pirate Dinosaurs
Go! Go! Go!"

And a **mighty** battle began.

Captain Flinn ducked
and grabbed the bottle
of tomato ketchup
out of the T. Rex's pocket.

"Take this, you smelly old
stink-head!" he yelled,
squeezing the bottle
with all his might.

"Aghh!"

screamed
the T. Rex.

He stumbled across the deck and fell with a great PLOP! into the water.

THEN there was a loud groaning noise.

"Take cover!" shouted Captain Flinn. "The sausage machine! It's about to explode!"

BOOOOOOOO

A jet of sludgy, wet sausage meat spurted out of the machine, splattering all the other Pirate Dinosaurs with gloopy, stinky, pink goo.

Out of the smoke appeared a very startled, bedraggled-looking Violet.

"You're safe!" cried Captain Flinn. "Come on, everyone . . . into the dinghy." Tom grabbed the oars and they quickly sped away.

In no time at all, Pearl,
Tom, Violet and Flinn
were back at the beach
where the rest of their class
were just finishing off
their drawings.

Miss Pie was inspecting the children's work.
"This is a very interesting picture, Tom," she said.
"It's the Pirate Dinosaurs, Miss," began Tom.
"That's the ship and that's the giant sausage machine.
And that's the Captain Tyrannosaurus Rex."

"Good Lord!" exclaimed Miss Pie. "What a lot of nonsense,
but you certainly win the prize for most active imagination!
now, everyone, it's time for lunch
and today we have your absolute favourite, Flinn . . .